A COVID ODYSSEY

A fictional COVID-19 pandemic story

Graham Elder

Copyright © 2020 Graham Elder

All Rights Reserved. No part of this publication may be reproduced, stored in, or introduced into a retrieval system, or transmitted in any form, or by any means (electronic, mechanical, photocopying, recording, or otherwise) without prior written permission of the copyright owner and publisher. For the purposes of a reviewer, brief passages may be quoted in a review to be printed in a newspaper, magazine, journal or by digital means.

This book is a work of fiction. The names, characters, businesses, organizations, events, places and incidents are the product of the author's imagination or are used fictitiously. Any resemblance to actual persons, living or dead, events, incidents or locales is coincidental and unintentional.

G.M. Elder Publishing
www.twodocswriting.com

Printed in Canada

ISBN: 978-0-9958907-3-2 (ebook)
ISBN: 978-0-9958907-4-9 (pbk)

I'd like to dedicate this book to all the healthcare workers around the globe who are putting their lives on the line daily, battling this disease. Your selfless sacrifices will echo through time and hopefully make this new post-pandemic world a better place.

PRESENT DAY

Saturday, March 21st, 2020

One hour before sunrise, I dragged a red 17-foot sea kayak down to the water's edge. My back-pack was lashed to the deck in front of the cockpit. There was a light breeze coming out of the west, and the only illumination was from my headlamp and sporadic lights on the shorelines. A little voice told me that this was madness of the highest degree. Sarah would not approve. No one would. I was a seasoned kayaker who'd tackled all sorts of extreme situations on the Great Lakes, but it was pitch black, and I had to cross a kilometer of shipping lanes on

St. Mary's River, where freighters sailed 24/7 with no predictable timing. Thousand foot freighters didn't move fast, but then, neither did kayaks.

Even with insulated booties, the water stung as I stepped in, breaking through a thin layer of ice at the water's edge. I stabilized the kayak with one hand and held my paddle with the other, carefully maneuvering my legs into the cockpit, almost tipping in the process. I hadn't slept more than an hour, and my nerves were raw with fear. My hands were shaking uncontrollably. Not from the cold, but from the terrified energy flowing through every atom of my being. What I was about to attempt was foolhardy at best, and it was turning my spine to jelly and my stomach into a constricted pit of acid. I desperately wanted to run back to our house, crawl under the covers of our bed. But what comfort would that give me? Knowing that my wife was in another bed, a hospital bed, fighting for her life.

I sat in the kayak, still holding on to a nearby rock for stability, checked my balance, rocking from side to side, feeling the kayak and water meld together, becoming one. I took a deep breath and looked up into the darkness, questioning myself once again and, in a moment of adrenaline ramped clarity, decided I couldn't live with myself if I didn't at least try to do everything I possibly could. As insane as this plan was, it was the only one that would allow me to get to Sarah in time.

I pushed away from the safety of shore, set my compass heading, aiming for the blinking red marker on the closest edge of the shipping lanes, and then settled into a comfortable paddle cadence.

There was no going back.

***

The darkness was a perfect cover, and I was running dead silent. A gentle breeze wafted the scent of seagull droppings from a nearby rock island on which towered the blinking red marker. I changed course and now targeted a white light beckoning from a beach servicing a trailer park on the Michigan side, about five-hundred meters from my position. Frigid late-March droplets slithered down my paddle on the upstroke splashing my face, heightening my focus. Despite an early thaw, patches of ice and small growlers still cluttered the river. I felt like a cat picking its way across an elegant dinner table ladened with fine crystal ware. Adrenaline bubbled through my veins, fueling each stroke. Sweat soaked the area between my shoulder blades as I crossed an invisible line demarcating the Ontario/Michigan border, gliding into the shipping lanes, into no man's land.

***

I was staring at ghostly reflections on the surface of the water, lulled by the rhythm of the waves, when I felt the propeller groan of a thousand-footer. As I looked upstream, towards the bright multicolored outline of the International bridge, the deafening blare of its horn – one short blast – tightened my gut into a Gordian Knot. The blast wasn't for me. Without some form of metallic reflector, my kayak was invisible to the freighter, just another molecule of water bobbing along the river. The blast was for another freighter approaching from somewhere downstream, letting her know that she was going to pass on her port side. Unbeknownst to either of them, I was caught in the crossfire. The fastest I'd ever pushed a kayak, by GPS, was 12 km/hr. I dug my paddle deep into the black water and pulled harder.

***

A hundred meters from shore, an eight-foot swell heaved me from behind, straining and twisting the kayak, pushing me forward. The south bound freighter had narrowly missed me, but its wake was my perfect storm. In the beginning, it was like surfing, almost fun. And then the crest of a wave caught my paddle, and the early spring waters funneling through St. Mary's river from Lake Superior swallowed me whole.

Fortunately, I was wearing my lifejacket, and I had a full wet suit. There was no chance I could right the kayak. Not in the dark, in these swells, in waters that rendered even your gloved fingers completely numb in seconds. The icy black depths of the river threatened to drag me under, but I held on to the kayak for buoyancy, until the wake from the freighter settled, and then detached my backpack and began swimming for shore. Although the backpack was an obstacle, I couldn't leave it behind. It was the purpose of my trip, my mission. I glanced back at the receding whale-like outline of the freighter, and swore. I was failing, and the love of my life would pay the price.

FOUR DAYS EARLIER

Tuesday, March 17th, 2020

"Sarah? Can you hear me?"

"Barely," the phone crackled. "Hang on ... I'll ... to the balcony. That better?"

"Much," I said, relieved. "Much better. What's happening? Shouldn't you be heading to the airport?"

"My stupid flight was cancelled again, rebooked for the day after tomorrow at 1 PM. Did my sister and the girls make it home okay?"

"Yeah. They said the connection was tight. Jenna is still waiting for her luggage. They all said they had a great long weekend. Invaluable learning, according to Trish." I smiled to myself. The only learning that happened on this girl's weekend – disguised as a pharmaceutical conference – was personal alcohol tolerance.

"Is Archie okay?" Sarah asked.

"He's great. We watched a contemporary double feature last night, Outbreak and Contagion. Things are starting to get pretty crazy out there, in the real world. I thought there might be some clues as to how all of this plays out."

"And?"

"Mmm, let's just say that if real life imitates the movies, we're in trouble. Hey," I asked gently, "how are you holding up? Have you heard of any cases at the resort?"

Her voice faltered just a little. "I'm okay, a little nervous. There's no one in the resort but me now, I think. They keep asking when I'm leaving."

TWO DAYS EARLIER

Thursday, March 19th, 2020

"Sarah, they just announced that they're closing all the US borders as of tonight at midnight. But you should be okay. Your flight is still with Air Canada this afternoon at 1 PM, right? And you only have the one connection through Chicago and then Toronto. Even if you get delayed again, Trudeau said that everything would be done to get Canadians home."

There was no response for an agonizing

amount of time, and then I heard a small, restrained cough. "Sarah? You there?"

"Mark, I'm not feeling too good. I'm achy all over, burning up, and I've got chills."

"And you've got a cough," I added, nervously.

"That just started this morning. Mark, I think I've got it – the virus. What the hell do I do? Regardless of whether the borders are open or closed, they won't let me on the plane like this, will they?"

I was torn. Part of me wanted to tell her to fake it. Take a gallon of cough syrup and a ton of acetaminophen, suck it up and get on board. She clearly had all the symptoms of the virus, though, and she would be spreading it like a sprinkler system throughout the plane. Sending it onward to every conceivable destination. Infecting the world. My wife – a Typhoid Mary.

I spoke slowly now, resigned. "No, Sarah. You can't go on a plane until you're better. You have to go to the nearest hospital and get tested and treated."

"You could drive down and get me," she said

weakly.

It was a straight 24-hour drive down and a 24-hour drive back. At best, it would be the most miserable time of our lives, at worst, things could turn terminal very quickly. “You still need to get checked ASAP. If you’re okay, then we’ll see.”

“I’m scared, Mark. Really Scared.”

“Everything will be okay. You’re young and in great shape. Whatever you’ve got you can fight it off. Do you hear me?”

“I hear you. I just wish you were with me.”

“I do too.” I could hear guarded sobs. “Love you, Sarah.”

My heart was racing and sinking simultaneously. I stared uselessly at my phone. My wife had COVID-19, and there was nothing I could do to help her.

***

“Where are you?”

"The resort organized a ride for me," Sarah replied. Her voice sounded strained, muffled. "They were happy to get rid of me, I'm sure. I'm at Cape Coral Hospital; I've been waiting for hours. I've never seen so many sick people, they just keep pouring in. I was super lucky to get here when I did and at least get a seat. It's crazy, Mark. Everyone's wearing a mask and gloves."

"Still burning up?"

"Yeah, plus I'm having a tough time catching my breath."

"That's new."

"I noticed it when we arrived at the hospital. I thought it was anxiety. Being here. It's like something out of a movie." She let out a long sigh. "Can you just ... talk to me, Mark. Get my mind somewhere else."

I paused, collecting my thoughts. I didn't want to talk about work, about the Emergency Room. The preparations being made. We only had a dozen community cases at this point, but we were digging in, getting ready. A lot had happened in the short time since she had left. Our city was completely shut down. Social distancing measures in place. All of this was nothing she needed to hear right now.

"I guess we'll have to make other plans for our anniversary next –"

"Mark, they just announced my number. Call you back."

***

Waiting has never been my strong suit. Some people are good at it, I'm not. It had been three hours, and I had tried calling multiple times and got nothing but her voicemail. There are only so many ways you can say "call me back." I looked into the eyes of our six-month-old Golden Retriever sitting on the couch next to me, his head on my lap. "What should I do, Archie? What *can* I do?" He smiled, licked my hand and then nudged my phone with his snout. It rang.

"Sarah?"

"Hellooo there, handsome," Sarah answered. She sounded far away, like she was in a wind tunnel. And she had that singsong voice, the one she gets after a half bottle of chardonnay.

"What's going on? You were going to call me back."

"Sorry, honey bunny. I think I fell asleep. They admitted me right from triage and then gave me something for anxiety, to help me breath more easily."

"Okay. That's good. It sounds like you have a mask on or something."

"I do. I'm getting oxygen. I heard the nurse say my 'sats were in the toilet'. That means my blood's not getting enough oxygen, right? I've heard you saying something like that to nurses on the phone."

She's getting worse.

"Something like that. Have you told the doctors about your asthma? They may need to give you your puffers. Actually, can you call for a doctor or nurse. I'll speak to them."

"You silly boy, Dr. Mark. I'm in a hallway. There's no call bell. My mask is connected to a looong tube that's goes to a biiig green canister on the floor."

"Sarah, there must be some way you can call someone?"

"They're so busy, Mark. The nurses and the doctors. They're running and running. They don't stop. And I don't have the breath to yell. I need to sleep. That sedative is really working. Knocking me out. Call you …"

"Make sure you tell them about the asthma … and that you have top notch insurance. Sarah? SARAH!"

***

Another three hours since Sarah's last phone call dragged by, each minute passing like a day in an emergency waiting room. I thought I was able to compartmentalize everything, but as I opened my hands, which had been clenched into granite hard fists, I noticed my palms etched with fingernail markings on the verge of oozing blood. After dialing the hospital repeatedly, I fully expected the redial button on my phone to give up. *I* was about to give up, when the first notes of a jazz version of "Over the Rainbow" sang from my phone. I had been so anxiously bored that I'd reset my ringer at least a dozen times, finally settling on one of Sarah's favorite tunes. I expected Sarah's name on the screen. Instead, it was her hospital.

"Dr. Spencer?" A male voice asked.

"Speaking."

"This is Dr. Fleming. I'm taking care of your wife here in the ER at Cape Coral Hospital. She asked me to call you, to give you an update. I understand you're an ER doc also, working in Northern Ontario."

"Yes, I am. Thanks for taking the time."

"Listen, I'm sorry to tell you, your wife's not doing well. She's currently on a rebreather mask,

50% O2. I've also given her a sedative, as well some acetaminophen for her fever. She's deteriorating quickly though. We've tested her for COVID-19, but the results are still pending."

This was a conversation I had with the family of patients every day. Now I was on the receiving end, and it cut deep. I fumbled for a moment, gathering my thoughts, pushing my feelings to the side.

"Will she need intubation?"

"Well, that's the problem, isn't it? We're a small community hospital with a limited number of ICU beds and ventilators. It's basically a war zone down here. Way more cases than we can possibly handle. We can't very well kick patients off our ventilators because someone else needs them. That would be a death sentence and an instant lawsuit. Our current mandate is to triage and save patients with the best chances of survival. This means those with minimal or no comorbidities. Now, your wife has asthma and diabetes. Also, her liver enzymes are elevated. Does she have liver disease? Maybe cirrhosis?"

What the hell is he talking about?

"Dr. Fleming, Sarah has mild asthma and only rarely requires puffers. She was just recently diagnosed with diabetes – *so recent that I had forgotten about it* – and has borderline high blood sugars easily controlled with her diet. She was at a conference over the past few days with her sister and some girlfriends. I suspect she was celebrating with a few drinks. There's nothing wrong with her liver. Hell, she runs marathons and is normally the specimen of health."

"Nevertheless, these co-morbidities are now on her chart. And at the moment, that places her down the list in terms of access to a ventilator."

"What about medical management?" I asked. "There are a number of medical therapies being trialed: Hydroxychloroquine, convalescent plasma, high dose vitamin C, new anti-virals like Camodesivir?"

"What little Hydroxychloroquine we have is

being kept for the sickest patients in the ICU. The newer anti-virals are being tested in the larger centers and not available. We did start her on an antibiotic, Azythromycin, as well as high dose vitamin C, but we have no idea if they really help."

"Damn it. So, all my wife has access to in your hospital is partial supportive therapy? That's crazy."

"I'm sorry, Dr. Spencer. We are doing our best with what we have. Look, I'm married also, and I can only imagine what you are going through."

He's delivered shitty news and now he's trying to connect with me, to make the medicine go down more easily. Right out of the playbook.

He continued, "From one ER doc to another, I'll do everything I can to help her. Okay?"

"Right. Thanks. Please call me if there's any change."

"Will do. Again, I'm really sorry." The line went dead.

I stood up and walked across our living room to a large bay window overlooking Ste. Mary's River where a large freighter was passing in the distance and an eager fisherman was trolling the waters in front of our house, deftly dodging small icebergs that were flowing downstream from Lake Superior. Less than a kilometer in the distance, I could see buildings, shipyards, and a trailer park making up the coastline of Michigan, USA. It was right there in front of me, but the border would be closed as of tomorrow morning.

My wife was getting next to no treatment for a disease that could kill her – I had to do something. I was a doctor. Sarah and her sister were both pharmacists who worked at our hospital. The pharmacy had recently acquired a batch of one of the new antiviral drugs. A plan began to germinate in the back of my mind.

YESTERDAY

Friday, March 20th, 2020

"Jenna, I need your help."

Sarah needs your help.

I was using Facetime. I needed Jenna to see me. See my desperation. But I also needed to be sympathetic. Sarah was Jenna's sister.

"You're sure she has it?" There were certain facial expressions that both Jenna and Sarah shared and the angry-surprised scowl was one of them. "Shit. That means I've probably got it. How could my own sister give me Covid?"

"Actually, Jenna, you may have given it to her.

It may just be that you have a longer incubation period. Also, you haven't had any symptoms, right? It's possible you're an asymptomatic carrier."

She sighed and closed her eyes. For just a moment, I saw tears begin to run with her mascara. And then, I was looking at a white ceiling fan. She had put her phone down on a table, and I could hear sobbing and then a choked, distant voice. "I guess it is what it is, and it doesn't really matter who had it first, does it? Poor Sarah, my baby sister, she's all alone …"

Nothing's more contagious than sorrow. I had a lump in my throat the size of my fist, so it was easy to let a full minute evaporate before I asked, "Jenna? You alright?"

She picked up her phone and attempted a smile. "Sorry, Mark. I just needed to process." She was more composed now. Her tears had been wiped away, leaving crusty streaks on her cheeks. "You must be worried sick. How bad is it? What symptoms does she have?"

"Fever, dry cough, shortness of breath," I rattled off, like I was teaching a medical student. "The big three." There were many other symptoms connected to COVID-19 that were being discovered daily, but these were the most common, the ones that made everyone suddenly back away from you.

"I guess if you throw in 'travel out of country', she's the classic case," I added.

I told them it wasn't safe to go. Dammit, I told them.

"And she has asthma and diet controlled diabetes, two risk factors." Jenna said. "She was needing her puffers over the weekend, and her diet certainly wasn't very controlled."

Sarah hadn't mentioned the puffers.

"I'm scared, Mark. I'm scared for her and I'm scared for me. I was with her the whole time. I've definitely been exposed."

"Jenna, you're healthy with zero risk factors. Chances are, even if you get it, you probably won't know. And if you do get sick, our new hospital is fully equipped. State of the art ventilators. Plus, as you already know, we have a stock pile of that new anti-viral study drug, Camodesivir, in house."

"Yeah, we're crazy lucky our I.D. specialist saw this coming," Jenna added. "Did you know he had a buddy actually doing a two-month fellowship exchange at a Wuhan level 4 lab in October and November. He's the guy we need to thank for the heads up."

Not likely, I thought to myself. Jenna obviously didn't know, and I wasn't going to tell her now. At the end of his rotation, he apparently had left the lab and volunteered to help at a local hospital. He contracted Covid and died shortly afterwards. They had lousy PPE. And he had lousy, unfair karma.

There was a long pause before Jenna said, "Mark, there must be something they –"

"Like I said, I spoke to Sarah's physician in Florida. It's a small hospital with very limited resources and no access to any of the new anti-viral meds. They are completely overrun with cases. I'm really not sure how much they can help her."

"Can we do anything from here?"

"From here? Nothing. You're in quarantine for fourteen days. It's not like we can Purolate the anti-viral meds to her."

Don't you get it, Jenna? There's no other choice. It's me...

"I think I have to go to her, Jenna. I need to bring Sarah that new antiviral – Camodesivir. It's the only chance she has."

"Wait. What about air ambulance, like Ornge? Surely her insurance company would rather look after her here – covered by our tax dollars – than run up a million-dollar hospital bill in Florida."

"I called them first thing after I got off the phone with her doctor. They said they would try, but with the high number of Covid patients needing repatriation, and with all the flights cancelled, they were really backed up. It could be 4 or 5 days, or more. She can't wait that long. She needs treatment now.

"Look, Jenna, I know I'm asking a lot. It's completely illegal and we'd be stealing from the hospital." I paused here, letting it sink in. We could both lose our jobs, our licenses, maybe even go to jail. Sarah, however, could lose her life. There was no decision to make here.

"Can you help me get it?"

"She was my sister long before she was your wife, Mark. Of course, I'll help.

"Almost everyone was at this conference." Jenna continued. "Most of the pharmacy department is in quarantine."

"Who's left? Can you call them? Make an arrangement?"

"There's David. He felt it was more of a girl's weekend. He was right. Lucky him."

"I have a shift at the hospital this afternoon," I said. "Tell him, I'm coming to get it. I'm planning to leave tonight, as soon as my shift is done. How will you convince him? Those meds are under strict lock and key right now."

"I'll tell him the truth. We pharmacy people are tight, like family, I don't think it will be a problem." She gave me a confident look that said, "One way or another, you'll get those meds."

"Alright. I'll leave it in your hands."

A few seconds of empty air passed, both of us staring away from our phones in deep thought, before Jenna looked at me quizzically, and asked, "Mark, I know you like adventure, but this is crazy, even for you. How do you plan on getting across the border? I hear they're not letting anyone through anymore unless it's essential services."

"This is pretty damn essential." I replied sternly.

"It's not me you have to convince."

"I guess I'll cross that bridge when I get to it."

***

I finished my shift at 6 PM in the ER. It was quiet, which had become the norm since the pandemic started and social isolation began. No one playing team sports meant no twisted ankles and broken wrists. Hip fractures and ruptured appendixes still made regular appearances but, because people were terrified of visiting a hospital, all the chest pains and dizzy spells seem to have disappeared. This was concerning, since they really hadn't disappeared, they just lay dormant, ready to progress to the next incurable level. I suspected the real cost of pandemic fear to our society would never be fully measured, except in unnecessary funeral expenses.

I changed out of my scrubs and took my mask off for the first time in eight hours. I inhaled deeply, the stale smell of breathing through a mask for an extended period lingered in my throat. I was anxious to get outside and breathe fresh air. In my briefcase, I carried the potential cure: a ten-day supply of Camodesivir. David had come through with no questions asked. He said it was a small amount of medication that could easily be "fudged" off the books. I imagined I saw a tear in his eye when he wished his best for Sarah. That was the first of many times I would break the law on this mercy mission, and I'd made David an accomplice.

When I got into my Highlander, I transferred the medications to my backpack. As I left the hospital parking lot, I tried to blank everything from my mind, except for the journey at hand. I had left Archie with my neighbours prior to my shift, good dog people that he got along well with. The stars seemed to be aligning nicely.

***

I entered the on-ramp where a large sign indicated that the border was closed, effective today – except for essential services. The question was: what represented essential services? I had reviewed a detailed list on their website, but I didn't quite fit into any category. This was my biggest worry, and I sucked at lying, especially to people with weapons.

As I crossed the International Bridge, I noted the steel factory was still up and running, the flames and smoke shooting high off the stacks. I quickly fell into line behind a caravan of four eighteen wheelers carrying essential goods. I was the lonely four-wheel vehicle on the bridge. We passed over the Ste. Mary's River Canadian and American lock systems and then a series of retirement homes on a peninsula as we approached the Michigan coast line. I shook my head. Retirement homes had become breeding grounds for Covid, death traps.

There was only one customs booth open. I waited patiently behind the trucks and took the opportunity to call Sarah. As expected, she didn't – couldn't? – answer. I left a message telling her that I was coming. Her doc in shining scrubs to the rescue.

The light turned green. It was my turn. My mask and gloves were in place. I rolled down my window and passed my passport to the customs official which he accepted with gloved hands. He also was wearing a mask, and he cut right to the chase.

"Please state your business in the United States."

I explained that my wife was critically ill in a hospital in Florida and that I had to go to her, to bring her back to Canada. Since I was a lousy liar, I decide to go with the truth, and nothing but the truth. This was a mistake.

"Sir, you are aware that only essential travel is permitted across this border as of today, in light of the COVID-19 pandemic." He added this last part, like I might have been emerging from some remote cave in the northern wilderness.

"Yes, of course." I replied courteously, nodding my head in the affirmative. "This is an emergency, for medical purposes."

He shook his head from side to side and held a plasticized paper in front of him, presumably so that I could see it. He mumbled under his breath and then read, "Under 19 U.S.C. 1318(b)(1)(C) and (b)(2), travel through the land ports of entry and ferry terminals along the United States-Canada border shall be limited to 'essential travel,' which includes, but is not limited to –" he ran his finger down the list until he found what he was looking for, "Individuals traveling for medical purposes (e.g., to receive medical treatment in the United States)." He looked up, as if everything was now perfectly clear.

"Sir. Are you, yourself, receiving medical treatment in the US?"

I stammered, "Well, no. My wife is. I need to visit her for, for medical reasons." I had decided that I couldn't say anything about the Camodesivir. It would bring up too many questions and would likely require some kind of special authorization.

"I'm afraid, according to this," he tapped the plasticized document, "your travel would not be considered essential. You'll have to turn around."

I lost it. I clamped both gloved hands on my door window's edge and shouted. "What?! My wife is dying in an American hospital, and I can't visit her? That's not considered a medical emergency? I'm a doctor for Christ's sake. I know what a medical emergency is. What the hell is wrong with you? Get me your fucking manager."

It is a mistake to swear at any well-armed authoritarian figure, particularly customs agents. Three officers carrying automatic weapons escorted me inside the main building to a small room where I was read the riot act about proper behavior towards customs officials. They agreed that the customs officer's interpretation of the travel restrictions was perhaps too literal, and that possibly I did qualify for entry on medical grounds. However, I had no documentation to prove that my wife was sick. I had behaved inappropriately towards one of their brethren and it was therefore impossible to be granted entry at present. I broke down in tears. The stress of the last 24 hours had caught up. As a conciliatory gesture, they allowed me to fill out some forms requesting special consideration and promised to get back to me in one to two business days. It was Friday evening, which meant I would hear nothing before Tuesday. I needed another plan, and I needed to become a better liar.

PRESENT DAY

Saturday, March 21st, 2020

Continued

I crawled up on the beach exhausted, the sand was hard and still mostly frozen. I lay there in the dark, in a fetal position, clutching my back-pack, deadened from the neck down. Standing would have been impossible, like getting up from a sofa after you've cut off the circulation to your leg. Slowly, painfully, the feeling came back, working its way outward from my core. Little sparks crackled throughout my body as nerves reignited, re-found their purpose. I opened my waterproof pack and removed a dry set of clothes, shoes and a heavy windbreaker. I had been a good boy scout back in the day. I munched on a power bar and downed a full bottle of water. I felt better. I was alive.

I reached deep into my pack and felt the outline of the watertight Camodesivir package. This gave me the boost I needed to push on.

I stood up and removed my wet suit. It was like peeling off a second layer of skin, maybe what a molting snake experiences. I left it on the beach. The wind had picked up on the shoreline, and I was freezing. I quickly donned my clothes, picked up my pack, and headed for the highway. I took a parting look at the river and realized that in the space of a day I had now broken the laws in two countries.

***

As the first hint of my shadow formed on the pavement in front of me, I felt a warmth massage my back, dissipating the remaining shivers that had taken up residence in my bones since escaping the water. It would be a blue-sky kind of late March day with higher than normal early spring temperatures. I killed an hour walking along the locks, watching other freighters lumber their way through, thinking about where, if anywhere, my kayak would wash up. And then I made my way to the Northern Michigan Car Rental where I sat on the curb outside the front door waiting, until a Ford F150 truck pulled up and stopped in front of me. The driver lowered his window and said, "You must be the fellow that left a message last evening looking to rent a car."

I stood up, stepped forward, smiled, gave a perfunctory wave, and replied, "Mark Spencer."

"Roger Nelson. Nice to meet you. Not much call for rentals these days. I damn near fell off my chair when I checked my messages this morning. Where are you headed?"

"Florida."

"Your online registration and paperwork all checked out. Pre-paid for two weeks. Good to go. So, you're Canadian, eh?" He grinned as he said this, exaggerating the "eh." A constant friendly source of amusement for our cross-border neighbours. He stifled a cough into the crook of his elbow. *Dammit,* I thought, *why didn't I put my mask on.* He continued, as he pulled his sleeve across his nose. "How the heck did you get across the border, anyway?"

I winced inwardly at that last comment, thinking *not easily*. "Sorry, can't say. Top secret." I grinned back at him, gently taking a social distancing step backwards, pretending to reach for my backpack.

He shook his head. "Probably military, or something, I'll bet. That's why you've only got that backpack and no luggage." He looked happy with himself, like he'd solved a Rubik's cube. "Anyway, tell you what. I gave you an upgrade to my favorite type of vehicle." At this, he tapped the outside door of his truck.

"That's very kind of you ... *eh?*"

He laughed out loud and then said, "Come

'round back. It's the red truck and it's been sitting for at least a week, so you don't have to worry about none of that virus stuff. I'll throw the keys to you from the back door."

And I'll be sure to wipe them down thoroughly.

***

I did the calculations in my head once again. It was a 23 hour and 46 minute drive to Cape Coral Hospital, according to Google Maps. If I added in three or four hours for a quick nap and a few pit-stops, best case scenario, I would be there tomorrow mid-day. I took a gulp of water, found a good radio station playing Bob Seger's "Against the Wind," set the cruise 10 miles/hour above the speed limit, and settled in. As expected, except for the occasional transport, the I-75 south was deserted. Two lanes of straight highway that seemed to go on forever, disappearing into the southern horizon.

After an hour, rhythmical divots in the highway told me I was approaching the Mackinac Bridge which spanned the common waters of both Lake Huron and Lake Michigan. I was approaching the toll booths on the north side and was curious as to how this would work. There was no way I could be more than six feet away and exchange cash in the usual manner.

There appeared to be one toll open, and there was one police car parked on the median between the north and south bound highways. I couldn't tell if the vehicle was occupied. I slowed to a crawl and put on gloves and a mask. I pulled into the toll booth and lowered my window. An older woman, also wearing a mask – inappropriately, with her nose exposed – waved at me and shouted, "Good morning," like everything was completely normal. She then extended a stick with a small reservoir on the end. I placed the four US dollars in it. She waved again, and the light turned green. I thought, *that was simple enough.* I paused for a moment, tempted to give her a short lecture on the proper wearing of her mask, but decided against it. I wasn't here to save everyone, and people rarely accepted unsolicited advice.

As I pulled out, I saw, in my rearview mirror, a police officer returning to his vehicle. He stopped mid stride, stared in my direction, and then brought a walkie-talkie to his mouth.

***

A half hour south of the bridge, a police cruiser pulled up behind and matched my speed. The car was close enough to scan my license plate. I realized I had a death grip on the steering wheel with both hands and attempted unsuccessfully to relax them. I glanced furtively back and forth between the road ahead and the rearview mirror, expecting the worst, which was soon delivered. Flashing red lights appeared. I took a deep breath, activated my ticker and drove onto the shoulder. I wasn't speeding significantly and, to my knowledge, I had done nothing wrong, other than maybe being the only non-transport vehicle on the road.

There was the requisite five-minute pause with the police car parked directly behind me during which I put on gloves and, this time, my N95 mask. I had brought two masks with me, a regular surgical mask and an N-95. My regular mask would probably do, but the literature wasn't clear at this point. Close proximity was a distinct possibility here, and it was better to be over protected than under protected. I reached for the registration papers from the glove compartment and an envelope from my backpack. An unmasked and ungloved male officer stepped out of his vehicle and approached my truck. I lowered my window, and his mustached face appeared, only a few feet away.

"Good morning," he said, as he angled himself to look inside the truck. "License and registration, please."

I quickly handed both to him, put on a smile he couldn't see beneath my mask, and then asked, "Is there a problem, officer?"

“Nice day for a drive. You’re coming from north of Mackinac Bridge.”

He stated this before he had even glanced at my driver’s license. I guessed the officer at the toll booth had radioed down. They were obviously watching the roads very closely.

“Yes. I’m coming from –”

“We are in a state of emergency here in Michigan.” Strong emphasis on Michigan. *Like I wouldn’t be aware of that*. He was staring intently at my papers. “No joy riding without a solid reason.”

He looked up, directly into my eyes. “You got a solid reason?”

I could feel the pulse in my neck bounding as I fumbled for the envelope. I replied, “Yes, I’m on –”

“Take off your mask, please.” He was standing less than two feet away. I hesitated and then simply said, “Social distancing. Do you mind moving back six feet, officer?”

Now *he* hesitated. I had challenged his authority. Finally, he almost imperceptibly shook his head and stepped one pace backwards. I removed my mask and he looked from my face back down to the license and up again. “You can put your mask back on, sir.”

I did exactly that and then he closed the gap again, and said, “What’s a Canadian doing on these roads travelling south?”

I delivered my rehearsed spiel, like my life depended on it. “I’m an ER doc from Ontario. I was asked to help out at Detroit Receiving Hospital. We have no significant cases yet and they’re over run. I have a colleague who works there. He asked for my help. I have this paper emailed from human resources.” I took the paper out of the envelope and handed it to him. He looked it over, occasionally glancing up at me. It was an easy thing to forge the letter, obtaining the hospital letterhead online, faking a signature. I had learned *something* from my experience with the Customs agents yesterday.

I knew there were a million holes in this story. A million ways he could trip me up if he asked the right question. All he said was, "No significant cases up your way?"

"Just a few in the community, nothing in the hospital yet. We're sitting around twiddling our thumbs."

He handed the letter back to me, rubbed his hands together taking a small step back, and asked, "Doc, how bad is this thing?"

"Bad enough that I'm heading to Detroit to help out."

He nodded his head. "Have a safe trip."

***

I was an hour past Detroit, and it was time to gas up. The Ford F150 was a great truck, with a big tank, but a terrible gas guzzler. The car rental guy may not have been doing me any favors. I found a small, deserted, no-name gas station just off the I-75 with two self-serve pumps. I gloved up and slid my credit card in. The pump asked for my five-digit zip code. Canadian postal codes are six digit alpha-numeric codes, such as J3R 1Z7. I tried entering the first five characters with no success. This was a problem, since the pump would not allow me to go any further, and I didn't particularly want to pay inside.

I donned my mask and walked over to the glass door of the small convenience store. The sign said open. I pulled on the handle, but the door was locked. I looked inside, through lightly tinted glass, and was startled enough to take an involuntary step back. Behind the counter was someone wearing a full yellow hazmat suit, including the headgear. On the shelf behind him at waist level, I could see what looked like a rifle. *I'm definitely not in Canada any-more.*

Hazmat Man moved around the counter and approached the glass door. Through the glass and through the face shield, I could see a youngish African-American man in his late twenties. He looked scared. *Scared of me?*

I showed him my visa card, and yelled, "I don't

have a zip code. I'm from Canada. What do I do? Can I pay inside?"

He shook his head and put his hand to his ear, like he couldn't hear me. He approached the glass door, propped his face shield up against it and looked at me with eyebrows raised.

The wind was picking up. I yelled, "No zip code. Canada. Pay inside." I pulled on the door and waved my credit card in the air. Eyes wide, he retreated two steps backwards and shook his head, waving his hands in front of him. He yelled something that sounded like, "Convert it," and then walked back to his counter where he sat down and rested one hand on the rifle. It was clear I wasn't getting inside. I walked back to my truck, the words "convert it" tumbling around my brain like clothes in a dryer. On a whim, I typed "convert postal code to zip code" into Google. The first hit revealed that all I had to do was use only the digits in my postal code and then add two zeroes. I smiled and said, "Thanks, Google."

As I was filling up the tank, a black Lab came from behind the gas station and began sniffing around the garbage can. He looked emaciated, starving. I remembered something. After I finished filling up the tank, I checked a small outside pocket on my backpack and found two dog treats from my last hike with Archie in the Fall. I crouched down, whistled, and yelled, "C'mon pup, over here. Come get a snack."

The dog was hesitant, at first. He had a mangled ear and looked like he'd been in a few scraps. He approached slowly, his tail curled, his teeth slightly bared and snout sniffing. I smiled and repeated, "Good boy," over and over. Finally, his snout was inches away from the snack in my hand. I gently commanded, "Sit." Which he did. I offered him the first snack, and he devoured it. His tail was now wagging. I gave him the second snack, pulled off one glove and patted his head, all the while whispering, "Good boy." The literature at this point had largely disproven any transmission between dogs and humans.

I suddenly heard a bell clinging, and the sound of a door opening. A voice bellowed at me from the gas station, "Stay away from my dog!"

Startled, I stood up, and the dog scampered away. I showed my open palms to Hazmat Man – who was carrying the rifle in his left hand. He closed the door, the bell ringing once more. I suspected he was worried I was going to give his dog Covid and then the dog would give it to him. *Ignorance and fear. A deadly combination. Lucky he didn't shoot me.*

I shook my head and walked over to the garbage can to discard my gloves. The mouth of the garbage can, however, was overflowing. It clearly hadn't been emptied in many days. Or weeks? I would imagine to Hazmat Man's eyes this garbage can was a cesspool of potential Covid. It was deeply ingrained in me not to litter, to respect the environment. Still, I wasn't bringing potentially contaminated gloves back inside my truck. I threw my gloves to the ground amongst hundreds of others that littered the surrounding area, and thought, *this is how the downward spiral begins.*

***

I was making good time, now in Kentucky, passing just north of Corbin, adjacent to the Daniel Boone National Forest. As soon as I saw the sign, the theme for the old television show, that my dad used to watch, popped into my ear and wouldn't let go, "Daniel Boone was a man, yes a big man ..." The scenery was majestic in the fading light as the sun set over a backdrop of towering white pines. Long shadows played across the highway and, if he hadn't dropped like a rock, I probably wouldn't have noticed him – the hitchhiker. Although I had no recollection of actually seeing him before he fell, my subconscious eye told me that one second he was standing there unnoticeable at the edge of the highway, and, the next, he was a heap of clothing on the pavement.

I passed the collapsed hitchhiker, stepping gingerly on the brake, still thinking about what I was going to do. I really didn't have time for roadside emergency medicine, I was on a mission. I craned my neck, hoping for some kind of movement, but I was still going too fast to be able to focus.

Maybe the next car or transport will stop?

I checked behind, and there were no vehicles anywhere. If enough time went by, it would be dark, and the next car might not see him.

Damn. No choice.

I pushed hard on the brake, activated my emergency flashers and pulled onto the shoulder. I drove backwards several hundred meters, until I was close enough to get a good look through the side mirror. There was definitely no movement.

I released a long sigh, slumped in my seat, and started running a differential diagnosis. Vasovagal episode? Epileptic seizure? Heat stroke? Delayed presentation of a head injury or a penetrating injury? Mechanical fall? Drug overdose? Alcohol intoxication? The possibilities were many.

I need to examine him.

I unbuckled, donned gloves and my N95 mask, and wished I also had a face shield and gown. Even though it was dusk, I put on my sunglasses. At least my eyes would have some protection. I opened the car door and stood at the side of my truck staring at him, or her. It suddenly occurred to me that the hitchhiker could be a woman. I mentally kicked myself in the ass. I was being biased and that could lead to poor medical decisions.

I approached him/her, knelt on one knee, and simply observed. The hitchhiker was lying supine, sporting a long, business-type black overcoat that looked fairly new over a white collared dress shirt. He had shoulder length black hair and a bushy beard that looked surprisingly well groomed.

Definitely male. Probably early sixties.

He had a small stud in his left ear and his eyes were closed. There was no obvious sign of foul play. The chest was rising and falling at a normal rate, a good sign. The sickly smell of days old alcohol was overpowering. A bad sign.

"Hello? Sir? Can you hear me? I'm a doctor. Can I help?"

I was preparing to administer a light sternal rub to wake him, when his eyes suddenly opened full moon wide. He sat up and said, "No need for that, I'm very much awake."

I stepped back, startled. He was indeed very much awake.

"I appreciate your offer of help, but really, I just need a ride."

His speech was clear and distinct. No slurring. In fact, he sounded well educated. He practically sprang into a standing position and brushed small pieces of gravel away from his overcoat. He looked down at me – he was quite tall – showed me a pearly white smile, and then said, "Well, then, shall we be off?"

"Uhhh … you're okay?" I asked.

"Oh, yes. I'm in perfect health."

"But ... you collapsed. On the side of the road," I stammered.

"Not really. You'd be surprised how hard it is to get a ride these days. What with this whole pandemic thing going on."

"But ... you smell like a brewery. I thought you were passed out drunk."

"Yes, of course. That was the intention. Someone is far more likely to give a helpless drunk a ride. We've all been there, right?" He gave me a wink with one of his big moon eyes and smiled again. "You seem like a good chap, though. No need to pretend."

"All you need is a ride?"

"If you please."

I wasn't sure if I was more relieved that I didn't have to deal with an important medical issue or more pissed off at being played for a fool. It had been years, maybe decades, since I'd picked up a hitchhiker, and now I remembered why. They were typically an odd bunch. And this one seemed odder than most. Despite being conned, I supposed

I couldn't very well just leave him at the side of the road at this hour of the night, although that's exactly what I wanted to do. I shrugged my shoulders, released a long exhale, and was about to run a hand through my hair when I noticed my glove. There was protocol to be followed.

"Stay here. I'll be right back."

He moved to follow, clearly unsure if I was going to drive off. "You won't leave me?"

"I'll give you a ride. Just – wait."

He seemed to accept this, not that he had much choice. I went to the truck, pulled out another set of gloves and my other mask, and waved him over.

"Can you put these on, please?" The tone of my voice was unnecessarily gruff. This was clearly a command and not a request. I didn't like being fooled, and he was slowing me down.

"That's really not necessary, you know. This whole pandemic thing has been greatly blown out of proportion."

"If you want a ride, put these on." My patience was waning.

He struggled for a moment, getting the mask on, fumbling with the tying of the knots blindly behind his head. It was a surgical mask I had "borrowed" from my hospital's surgical department. Better quality than the standard ear looped mask. Finally, I said, "Turn around. I'll tie it for you."

He even had some difficulty putting on the gloves, although they were perhaps a size too small. Still, he was really beginning to irritate me.

"My apologies. I've never worn this kind of mask or these kinds of gloves before. In fact, I'm not sure I've ever worn a mask before."

Well, you'd better get used to it. It's the future.

He climbed into the passenger seat, buckled up and settled in. I watched him adjust the seat, play with the ventilation, raise and lower the window, and could only think of all the time I would have to waste sterilizing and wiping down everything he had come into contact with. I clenched my eyes shut for a moment, willing him to go away, before I asked, "So, where can I drop you off?"

***

It was approaching 7 PM and almost completely dark. A low-lying fog had moved in quickly and my brights were no longer effective. I had to rely on regular headlights, and it was giving me tunnel vision. Fatigue was setting in, as well. I thought, *it might actually be good to have someone to talk to.*

"Do that often?" I asked, after a long uncomfortable period of silence.

"No," the hitchhiker answered. "I try to reserve that particular act for desperate moments. As I mentioned earlier, with this whole –" here, he raised the middle and index fingers on each hand in air quotes, "*pandemic thing,* the roads are quite barren and what few vehicles do pass are much less likely to stop for travelers.

"I had been waiting several hours for a ride,

but everyone bypassed me. The sun was setting, so I had to resort to ... old tricks."

"Well, it certainly worked." My nostrils flared just a little as I gave him a short, nasty glare.

"Hmmm, my apologies for that. Would you have stopped otherwise?"

"Doubtful."

"My point exactly. Tell me," he asked. "Do I detect a slight Canadian accent?"

"Yes, I'm from Ontario. Yourself?"

"I'm from these parts, here and there." By the subdued glow of the dashboard, I could see his hands pointing at the unseen passing landscape.

"You seem very well dressed. Are you a business man?"

"People are much more inclined to give you a ride if you look presentable and non-threatening." He chuckled as he said, "I am definitely not a business man." He then paused, as if he'd come to some sort of decision, "In fact, I'm a full-time intellect and writer."

Seriously?

"A full-time intellect?" I repeated, eyebrows raised. "Can't say I've come across that job description before." *And I've come across a lot of job descriptions in my ER career.* "Does it pay well? Being a full-time intellect."

"You attempt to mock me, sir. What is your name?"

I could see no harm in telling him. "Mark. Dr. Mark Spencer. I work in the ER. It's one of the big reasons I stopped to check on you."

"A doctor." He said this as if he was spitting out a mouth full of iodine. "Fancy yourself an intellect as well, then, do you?"

"I read a lot." I wasn't sure I liked the direction this conversation was going, but at least it was keeping me awake at the wheel. "It's part of the job to keep up to date."

"Exactly. You read mostly, or only, medicine. At best, you are a subspecialized intellect. There is a world of information to be absorbed. You are barely scratching the surface. If you want access to all of that knowledge, you must be a full-time intellect, as I am."

Well, he's got me there. I barely have time to read my journals.

"But, how does one afford to be a full-time intellect?" I asked.

"With so much astounding information available, how can one afford not to be?"

As an ER doc, I typically had thirty seconds to get someone's story. With this fellow, it was like dragging an anchor through a keyhole. Sometimes you had to ask the direct question. "How do you earn a living, Mister – Sorry, I still don't know *your* name?"

"Typical physician. Treating me like a slab of meat. God forbid you should see me as a real human being. A real person. Take an interest in who *I* am, as opposed to just the problem I'm presenting with."

Clearly, he has had issues with the medical system in the past. I was going to change the subject, but he was one step ahead.

"Why is a Canadian doctor driving south, through Kentucky?" He asked.

Again, I could see no harm in telling him. "My wife was at a conference in Cape Coral, Florida. She got sick. Covid. She's in the hospital there and they're not doing much for her. I'm bringing something to help. I hope."

"A medication?"

"Yes. A new anti-viral. A study drug."

"Which one?"

Like he knows about the latest antiviral study drugs?

"Camodesivir."

"Pfft! Garbage. Doesn't work. Can't work. It's a combination drug. Not particularly good at any one thing. Given enough time, the virus will overwhelm it with ease. Big pharma did a good job marketing that one. Not to mention potential deadly side-effects."

I was taken aback. Some of what he said was

true, but the early, independent, non-pharma associated studies, still showed very promising results.

"That's your opinion. But you're not a doctor, or a scientist, are you?"

"Ha, I am certainly not."

"You did say you were a writer?"

"I've written 127 books in all genres and topics."

"That's incredible. Is that how you generate an income? Anything I would recognize?"

"Doubtful. I don't publish."

"Hmmm, I've heard the traditional publishing industry is notoriously difficult to break into." I added, "Have you thought of self-publishing?"

"No. You misunderstand. I have no interest in publishing my work."

"Wouldn't you want to see the effect your work has on people?"

"I have no interest in what people think of my Canon. I write because it pleases me to write."

His own personal Canon? Wow! What can you

say to that?

"You still haven't told me your name." I asked.

"I haven't told you many –"

It came out of the fog. I swerved instinctively. We felt a heavy impact to the front of the truck. I slammed on the brakes, and we skidded to a stop.

***

Both of my white knuckled hands were welded to the steering wheel. If I checked my pulse, I would probably be in V-tach. I closed my eyes, inhaled deeply, and then asked, "You okay?"

"Yes. First class. I suspect it was a deer." He looked a little shaken, but otherwise fine. "You should probably check on it." He was very didactic, almost as if this happened to him all the time.

"You're right." I let out a long sigh, unbuckled, and then turned off the engine, leaving the headlights on. I activated the flashers. My hand hovered over the keys as I opened the door. "Coming?"

"No. Thanks. I don't do well with blood and guts. That's your department. Don't worry, I won't take off with your truck or lock you out."

He had read my mind. I hesitated. It is a very small-town Canadian thing to be overly trusting of people, and as much as it seemed absurd to leave a complete stranger – a hitchhiker – alone in my truck *with* my keys, I couldn't help it. "Okay. No problem. You stay here."

I reached into my backpack for my headlamp before stepping out of the truck and into a heavy fog that clung to my face, like cobwebs. I circled around to the front of the truck, standing in the beam of the headlights, and found a large dent in the right front wheel well area. There was also a small trace of blood on the bumper.

Shit. There goes my damage deposit.

I scanned the surrounding area with my headlamp, looking for the animal or a trail of blood. I even checked under the truck. A shiver ran through me, both from the chilled, dampness of the air and the shock of the impact. Had it been a moose, I realized, I wouldn't be standing here.

I walked into the opposite lane, towards the other side of the road, and found a small patch of fresh blood on the asphalt. It had definitely gone this way.

Was it dead? Wounded and dying? Did it run off with just a small cut and a bad bruise?

As I listened intently for animal sounds in the bush, I looked back at the truck, and felt distinctly more uneasy the further I moved away. *What the hell am I doing? What will I even do if I find it?* I had to think about Sarah.

I made up my mind. I slow jogged back to the truck and, just as I arrived, heard the click of door locks engaging. *WTF?* I pulled the door handle with no give. I was about to lose my shit, when I heard the door lock click again. I opened the door and glared at the hitchhiker.

"Apologies. I saw you running for the truck and thought I was unlocking it for you. My mistake."

Full-time intellectual, my ass.

***

The fog had lifted and with it the darkness from my encounter with the animal a half hour earlier. We were bantering conversation about once again, in a similar fashion of question/deflection, question/parry. The hitchhiker had a lot to say, but wasn't one to divulge much about himself. The truth is, he was a fascinating gentleman and the time was flying by. I still, however, had no idea why he was on the side of the road this night.

"You never told me what you were doing in Corbin."

"I'm travelling from Lexington to visit a sick brother in Knoxville." Straight to the point. He seemed to be warming to me.

"Not Covid, I hope."

"Humph, it would hardly matter if it was."

I cocked my head to the side, waiting for more.

I knew we would end up in this pandemic conversation eventually, but he didn't seem quite ready yet. I changed course once more. "Why are you hitchhiking?"

"Why not hitchhike? There are 227 million people with driver's licenses in this country. Why do we need any more?"

"Hmmm, lost your driver's license, eh? Seizure disorder? Alcohol?"

"You don't have any water, do you?" *Another deflection.* Probably deserved. Sometimes the inquisitive doctor in me had difficulty knowing when to hold back.

I reached into my backpack, pulled out the last of my two water bottles, unopened, and passed it to him. He lowered his mask, unscrewed the top, took a long gulp and tried to pass it back to me. "No thanks. It's yours, now."

"Ahh, the Covid thing. I keep forgetting." He put his mask back into position. "This device is very tiring to breathe through."

How does the great full-time Intellect and writer forget about one of the greatest pandemics to decimate the earth in the last one hundred years? "Okay, I'll bite. What's your *intellectual* take on the COVID-19 pandemic. Why don't you think it's a big deal?"

"I simply never got a driver's license."

"Sorry?" I asked. He was staring out of his window. There was nothing to see.

He turned his gaze towards me. "You asked me why I was hitchhiking. I never learned how to drive. Like owning a smartphone, I didn't think it was necessary."

"Wait. You don't know how to drive, and you don't own a smartphone?"

"Never have. It's an unnecessary luxury that continuously eats away at the limited time we have on this planet. Think of what more you could do with two, three or four more hours per day – the time that you spend on your phone. Think of how many more lives you could save."

"I often use the phone to save lives. To look up information."

"And yet, for a hundred years, we had no such devices and somehow lives were still saved. You are losing part of your mind to this portable brain. Soon human beings will not be able to function without them."

"How is it different from laptops or regular computer terminals?" I asked.

"We have not evolved sufficiently to be continuously part of the collective consciousness that is the internet. You have to be able to walk away from it. To detach."

"It's the future," I replied.

"That doesn't make it a good future, or the right future."

He continued, "The smartphone is the most savage marketing tool ever invented. There are 300 million in the USA, and over 5 billion in the world. You asked me why I don't think the pandemic is such a big deal?"

Uh-oh, here it comes.

"Because, like a bad flu, it's just another virus. The only difference is, it's one of the best advertised viruses in the history of humanity, courtesy of the internet, and brought to you never-endingly by the smartphone."

***

We sat in silence for a while. I really couldn't think of anything I could say that would counter the hitchhiker's last statement. He was partly right. The SARS-CoV-2 virus did have the most intense marketing campaign of any virus, ever. But that didn't make it any less dangerous.

"Here is good," he said, unexpectedly.

"Excuse me?"

"You can let me off here." We were stopped at a light, just north of Knoxville.

"Right here, on the highway? If it's not far, I could pull off and take you to the door."

"Not necessary. My brother lives a short walk from here."

I abruptly came to realize that I was going to miss this eccentric man's company during the remainder of my trip. "Well, I hope your brother gets better soon."

He removed his glove and reached for a handshake. I actually considered it for moment – removing my glove and shaking his hand. Skin on skin contact. Something I hadn't done in quite some time. Critical thinking prevailed, though, and I kept my glove on.

"Still not ready yet, are you?" He said. "You know, it's the *fear* of the virus that will cause the most profound changes, not the actual virus itself."

He reached into his inside jacket pocket and handed me a business card. "Email me when you get home. To let me know how your journey turned out." He smiled, closed the door and waved to me through the window as he made his way onto a sidewalk and then disappeared into the darkness. The traffic light had long since turned green. I looked into my rearview mirror and there was no one in sight. I turned on the interior cabin light and curiously looked at the business card, looking for a name. On one side, there was an email address, and on the other, all it said was, "The Hitchhiker."

***

On the southern outskirts of Knoxville, Tennessee, my mind was still reeling from my conversations with The Hitchhiker when my gut began to gurgle. I hadn't eaten anything substantial since yesterday. I needed to look after myself, "a little self-care," as Sarah would say. My plan was to pull over at a rest station – they were still open for truckers – and sleep a few hours at some point, but I needed food in my belly first.

I eased off the I-75 and drove almost ten miles looking for a takeout joint before I found something. Bob Seger was on the radio again, this time playing

"Turn the Page," hauntingly appropriate as I pulled into a truck stop type mom and pop diner, which, given the number of cars and trucks in the parking lot, was clearly open. I was relieved, but at the same time concerned. *Shouldn't they be in some sort of lock-down? Shouldn't it only be take out?* I parked a safe distance from everyone else – my little parking spot island – and donned my N95 and gloves. I checked my phone for messages but, for whatever reason, my phone had no reception.

I pushed an old wooden door open into a small vestibule and a bell jingled. On the walls, there were numerous adds: tractor rentals by the hour from Glen, Junes best blueberry pies, missing dogs, cats and even a cow. Nothing about Covid. The air was thick with the aroma of bacon and burgers, the sounds of dishes, cutlery, and conversation. I pushed a creaky second door open into the main restaurant. It was much bigger than expected and completely packed. A haze of heat seemed to be hovering at eye level. People were elbow to elbow, no masks or gloves, passing towering plates of family style food with sweaty hands. If I were a coronavirus, I would want to live here, in this place.

A hush came over the predominantly plaid dressed patrons. With my white bulbous mask and blue gloves, I stood out like the grim reaper at a wedding. Heads turned in my direction and some started laughing. Laughing at me. The cat calls and jeers came from everywhere at once.

"We don't need that in here."

"Take it off or get out."

"Take your conspiracy bullshit elsewhere."

I was paralyzed. Not with fear, but with confusion and incomprehension. *My conspiracy bullshit?* A waiter quickly came to me. "Look, we don't want any trouble. You're obviously from away. People here, in this town, they don't go for the whole virus thing that's on the news. Your welcome to stay, if you take off the mask and gloves."

My mind swirled with indecision. It was as if he'd asked me to remove my oxygen tank a hundred fathoms under the sea, or go bare handed during a bloody procedure on an HIV patient.

"Any chance there's another take out restaurant nearby, one with more relaxed rules?"

"All closed, everywhere. We're special here," he replied, tilting his head ever so slightly, as if to say I was very lucky to be in his establishment.

Every ounce of common sense and professional training told me to turn heel and leave. Sometimes, however, the body controls the mind. At this point, the sizzling, greasy aromas had released a flood of enzymes into my stomach. It was like I was being eaten up from the inside. And then, my mind started justifying what my body wanted.

It's not like you've ever seen a real case of COVID-19. You've only read about it, everywhere. An infodemic that has infected all aspects of the news, the internet, social media, and daily conversation. Maybe it really is nothing more than a bad flu? Maybe this whole trip to help Sarah is ridiculous, a product of your over-active and over informed imagination?

I shook my head, trying to clear my thoughts and jump-start my logical mind. But to no avail, it wouldn't turnover. I stood there like a statue, with my confusion, like sweat, dripping out of every pore. *What should I do?*

I spotted a compromise, an empty table in the corner with at least six feet of clearance around it. I bargained. "No problem, I can take them off. Okay if I sit at that table over there?"

"Of course. Follow me."

As I took the mask and gloves off, I heard a few claps and whoops. Like they had made another convert to their cause. I felt like I had entered a parallel universe. *What the hell am I doing here?*

I sat down hesitantly at the table and the waiter placed a menu in front of me. He asked, "What'll you have to drink?"

With the waiter hovering over me, right next to me, I worked through all the breeches of protocol in my head that would be required to eat this meal. Covid fomites – materials that can carry infection –

were a real thing and included objects like tables, chairs, knives, forks, glasses and menus for up to three days after exposure to the virus.

The literature on food was unclear. Certainly, it could live on the plastic or cardboard packaging, but no one knew for sure about food itself, the thing you were putting straight into your body, down the gullet that lived right next to your trachea which led straight to your lungs, the most well-known target of Covid. And then there was the waiter with his hands all over everything, the people around me, the ATM machine or cash exchanged at the end of the meal. The list was infinite, overwhelming all possibilities of enjoying this meal.

Was I becoming completely paranoid? Was I really the crazy one here? The outlier?

I closed my eyes, came to a decision and then stood up. I looked at the waiter, put my mask and gloves back on, and briskly walked out the way I came in. A little hunger was one thing that wouldn't kill me.

***

I snoozed for three troubled hours in my truck at a rest station a few hours south of Knoxville, where apparently COVID-19 wasn't a real thing. All the while trying to make sense of what had happened in the diner. In my dreams, the story was a simple one: I was hungry and I walked into a cool, fun, normal roadside diner where everyone was enjoying good food and good conversation. And then, I panicked and ran. They weren't the problem, I was, with my silly mask, gloves and attitude. What was wrong with me? When I awoke, a little bit rested, I was thinking more clearly – *maybe there isn't any coronavirus in Knoxville, Tennessee ... but there will be.*

As I rolled along, now 15 mph above the speed limit, with no police and still only the occasional transport truck, the midline stripes on the highway became a hypnotic blur and my mind started to wander. I hadn't spoken to Sarah in almost 3 days and I was getting anxious. What if I was too late? What if she was already –

A tired tear escaped into the corner of my eye. This was a bad path to go down. I moved Sarah to a protected space in my mind where she would be safe for the remainder of the journey, stepped on the accelerator, and then adjusted the cruise to 20 mph over the speed limit.

***

The sun was on the rise off my left shoulder for a couple of hours before being smothered by a day's worth of clouds. Google Maps told me to get off at the next exit. I had been on the I-75 for too long and was glad for the change. I was less than an hour from the hospital. I followed the mechanical voice's every recommendation, first on to the U46 Tamiami Trail for 25 minutes, and then onto Del Prado blvd, a straight run to the Cape Coral Hospital. Google Maps had me within five minutes of my destination when traffic started to build. It was just past 11 AM on a Sunday, typically a very quiet time. In fact, given the situation back home, where people were avoiding the hospital like the plague, I anticipated driving in to a nearly empty hospital parking lot. Traffic had now come to an almost complete standstill just a few minutes from the entrance to the emergency.

What the hell is going on?

A parking spot on the side of the street opened up, and I quickly pulled into it. I then opened the sunroof and stood on my seat. At first glance, it appeared the circus had come to town. There was a large tent standing in front of the Emergency Room entrance. I suspected this was a temporary triage tent erected to accommodate higher than normal volumes. A place where patients would be screened for Covid and determined to be hot (suspected of having Covid) or cold (unlikely to have Covid). From there, patients would be provided masks and gloves and then marched into appropriate zones in the Emergency Room. At least, this was how it was set up in our hospital back home.

In addition, there was a Fox news truck, reporters, a police squad car, hospital security guards and a group of demonstrators carrying signs with variations of "COVID-19 is a lie," "Fake Crisis," and "Land of the Free." I was astounded. Florida wasn't even in lockdown yet and protesters were hitting the streets. I could only imagine what it would be like a month from now.

I had read of the various alternate theories online, that Covid numbers were all wildly distorted by government agencies and completely unreliable. The more conspiracy like *Plan*demic – that COVID-19 was a custom-made virus designed to eliminate the middle class. That effects of COVID-19 were propagated by electromagnetic waves from the new 5G towers. So much talk online and on social media. It could infest your brain, if you let it. The worst kind of ear worms that even evidence-based mindfulness had difficulty resisting. I thought back to my experience at the diner in Knoxville with a clear mind and a shiver ran up my spine. Critical thinking was the only way to cut through the noise.

Everything was congested right up to the entrance of the Cape Coral Emergency. No masks, no gloves and no distancing. There were shouting matches, even a little bit of pushing. As I stood there, a man and a woman dressed in camo outfits and carrying rifles entered my peripheral vision walking towards the hospital on the sidewalk next to my truck. I flopped to my seat and sank as deep into it as I could. I had a thing about weapons. They scared the crap out of me, particularly after a one month fellowship rotation I had done in Detroit. A bullet is not concerned with human life.

I formulated a simple plan. I would find another entrance, away from all the commotion. I checked myself in the visor mirror. I definitely looked scruffy: black hair a little wild, a couple of days' beard growth. I poured some water from a bottle and smoothed things over. It would have to do. I donned my N95 and gloves, grabbed my backpack, walked around to the side of the hospital and quickly found an alternate entrance. There were two security guards, both in full PPE and a large sign that said, "NO VISITORS."

"Hi," I said, my voice nervously dry. "I'm Dr. Spencer. I'm here to see my wife. She's admitted to the Emergency department."

"ID badge, please." The smaller of the two guards said.

"I'm not from here," I said. I was about to continue that I'd driven all the way from Canada overnight, but realized that it might spark some concern, coming from out of country. "I'm from out of town."

"I'm sorry, Doc. You should know. No visitors allowed for any reason. Only staff and patients."

"Look," I pleaded, "My wife was at a conference. She's really sick. She's got Covid. She might be dying. I've got to see her."

The larger of the two guards dug into his pocket and pulled out a small business type card. "Call this number. They make special considerations. Particularly since you're from out of town and a doctor. Shouldn't be a problem. They'll get you on this list." He pointed to a paper loaded clipboard resting on a small desk.

I stepped back with the card in hand and muttered, "Fuck," under my breath. Before I turned to leave, I asked, "How long do you think this will take?"

He answered, "It *is* Sunday, and they are busy as all heck in there. This list comes out twice a day, so ... probably not until tomorrow morning. Sorry."

I muttered, "Fuck," under my breath again. "Okay, thanks." *Now I need a more complicated plan.*

***

I sat in my truck, frustrated, attempting to come up with a new plan, while watching this small, but passionate, demonstration unfold in front of me. How could their thinking could be so different from mine? I remembered the feelings that washed over me at the diner in Knoxville, the peer pressure that succeeded in making me question my scientific principles, even if only for a second. How hard it was to take a stand – literally to stand up and walk out. A small part of me admired these demonstrators. They believed in something, and they were making it known. That took guts.

I called Sarah's phone again with no luck. The ER put me on a never-ending hold. As I listened to the elevator music, I scrolled through the news feeds on my phone. New York City had been in lockdown for several days with their case numbers rising sharply. Headlines were all over the map: infringement on civil liberties, damage to the economy, over reaction by state governments. It appeared to me that the coronavirus was slowly becoming a misguided and deadly political weapon.

A group of hospital staff dressed in scrubs caught my eye as they walked pass my truck. I shut off my phone – as with previous times, I knew I was never getting through to the ER – and poked my head through the sunroof. The hospital staff was trying to go to work and was being blocked by the boisterous crowd. The police escorted them in and suddenly plan B took shape in my mind.

I pulled on my scrubs and fished my own hospital ID out of my backpack. It looked completely different from the ID badges I had noticed on the security guards at the side entrance. I put the lanyard over my head and then tucked my ID badge through the V neck in my scrubs to hang down in front of my chest, hidden from prying eyes. It had a cold, plastic feel to it. Next, I dug for the Ziploc bag of Camodesivir vials in my backpack. My plan was to hide it in the side pocket of my scrub pants. But I couldn't find it. Where the hell was it?

I picked up the pack and turned it upside down, shaking it until every last thing had fallen out onto the passenger seat. I opened all of the smaller pockets, knowing it couldn't be there. I searched behind and under the seat. I searched the entire cab. Where was it? I hadn't touched the Ziploc bag of medication since I had buried it deep in my pack at home, and I definitely remembered feeling it there when I changed out my clothes on the beach, what seemed like an eternity ago.

The realization struck me like a knife to the heart. Betrayal!

I cried out, "The fuuucking Hitchhiker."

When I was outside, checking on the deer. He must have rummaged through my pack and taken it. Why? Dammit. Why would he do that? Why would he steal the only hope my wife had?

Now, I was empty handed. I had nothing that could help her. This was the worst possible failure. The whole trip, for nothing. I sunk my head in my hands and sobbed. Sobbed until I could no longer see through the tears. Why had I been so careless? Why had I left my backpack alone with a total stranger I'd only known for an hour. What was I thinking?

Anger was starting to overcome me and flood my thinking. I began punching the steering wheel, over and over, until sweat mixed with the tears and I was exhausted. I sat there, spent. Nothing left in the tank but misery. I took a very deep breath, closed my eyes, and performed a short meditation to compose myself and get my shit together. Sarah was here. I was here.

I opened my eyes, took a large swig of water, opened the truck door with renewed determination and then headed for the crowd blocking the main Emergency entrance.

Sarah still needs me. And I need her.

The crowd was my perfect diversion. As I neared the protest, several gun toting people accidently bumped up against me. I fantasized about taking the gun and tracking down The Hitchhiker. If Sarah died, I would do it, I decided. Track him down and ...? I took another deep breath, and tried to focus.

I tapped a police officer on the shoulder and told him who I was and that I was going on shift. He held me there for a minute as a second group of staff formed around me. We were herded like celebrities through a group of paparazzi. A camera even flashed from one of the reporters. There were half a dozen security guards at the entrance checking ID's. My hand was holding up my lanyard with my ID badge still tucked under the front of my scrubs, well hidden. When the security guard asked for ID, there was just enough confusion for me to point to another guard and say, "He checked me already." I moved my hand in such a way that it looked like I had just placed my ID back under my scrubs. He waved me through.

Now I had to find Sarah.

***

I looked through a small window into the main section of the Cape Coral ER, and it was indeed a war zone. Stretchers lined every wall. The staff were all wearing full PPE. I ducked into a changing room and put on a gown, scrub cap, a new N95 mask and face shield. I wanted to fully fit in and be as invisible and unrecognizable as possible. I entered the main ER through two large swinging doors and was immediately assaulted by a cacophony of sounds: bells, beeps, oxygen flow, voices, crying, yells, the shuffle of feet, squeaky gurney wheels, and on and on. It felt just like my hospital on a busy day.

This was a relatively small emergency room and, as was often the case in small hospitals, the staff looked like a tightly knit group. If I started asking around for Sarah, it would certainly arouse suspicion. I may have been able to convince the security guards that I belonged here, but it was doubtful that I could fool the regulars.

I dialed her on my phone once more, maybe hoping to hear a ringtone. No luck. I texted her, in case she had the rebreathing mask on and couldn't talk. No reply. There were several possibilities: she was asleep, her phone was dead, or she was –

I began strolling the hallways, trying to absorb their setup. They seemed to have a hot zone of COVID-19 suspect or positive patients – which I was standing in now – and a cold zone in the back, through another set of doors. Sarah would certainly be somewhere here. I looked from patient to patient, but it was hard to make out facial features from outside the rooms looking through a window, particularly since they were all wearing oxygen masks. Still, I saw nobody that even remotely resembled my wife, at least from afar. I approached the back of the hot zone and noted two gurneys with body bags blocking a restroom entrance. My stomach lurched and heaved. I had last talked to her just over three days ago, there was no way …

I circled the whole hot zone again, probing a little deeper this time, going into rooms and making excuses if the patient was awake, "Oops! Sorry, wrong room." Finally, I found myself in a Covid positive room with a patient who resembled my wife enough that I had to get a closer look at the face under the oxygen mask. As I moved to her bed side, I realized she was trying to say something but couldn't get the words out. Her face and fingers were turning a faint tinge of blue and purple. Contracted muscles on either side of her neck looked like violin strings as she struggled to catch her breath. Her eyes were wide, as if she were staring into the maw of death itself.

This woman is desaturating. Why isn't her pulse oximeter alarming?

I could see nothing amiss with the monitors other than they looked ancient, a mishmash of older equipment jury-rigged for the occasion. I flung open the door to her room, ran into the hallway and yelled, "CODE BLUE." A team of nurses quickly arrived and assessed her. One of the nurses yelled, "Mrs. Anderson, we're going to insert a tube to help your breathing."

I was relieved that it wasn't Sarah, and I should have backed away immediately and disappeared before anyone realized I wasn't on staff. Professional curiosity, however, got the better of me. This was the first real COVID-19 patient I had ever seen. Her respiratory distress was horrifically profound. I had seen autopsy pictures of Covid lungs in journals: "Lungs like rubber" was a typical description used. It was no wonder Mrs. Anderson couldn't breathe. I thought back to the protestors outside and wanted to warn them.

No matter what you think, COVID-19 is deathly real.

Another doctor arrived and began a rapid intubation protocol. Medications were administered through her IV and an endotracheal tube was expertly placed. I stood in the background near the door watching, listening, wanting to help.

The doctor asked, "Why the hell didn't the oxygen probe alarm?"

A nurse answered, "It's one of the old ones. We dug it out from the back of the supply room. It must have failed." She shrugged her shoulders. "It was that or nothing."

"She would have been better off with nothing." Under the mask, I could imagine he was glaring at her. "At least someone would have been checking on her more closely."

Tempers were clearly running high in this war-like environment. The doctor looked at me and yelled, "You, whoever you are, tell the desk we need a ventilator and an ICU bed stat. And don't take any shit from them. Tell them we need it NOW!" I heard him mumble as I was leaving, "Can't tell who anyone is anymore with all this fucking PPE ..."

I ran to the nursing desk, relayed the message and then ducked around a corner, out of site, and waited. Within minutes the team was escorting Mrs. Anderson on a gurney towards an elevator.

When all the excitement had settled, I realized I was no further ahead. Where was Sarah? I circled the hot zone once more. Could she be in the ICU? Dr. Fleming had said she likely wasn't a candidate for a ventilator because of her comorbidities. That she was far down the list. Could something have changed?

I'm running out of time.

At this point, I was confident that my wife was

not in the hot zone. Did they move her to the cold zone? Fatigue threatened to overwhelm me, and I was having more and more difficulty focusing. This journey had bent my mind. I was no longer thinking straight, and I was drowning in hesitation. Physicians are trained to anticipate the worst possible outcomes. I was drawn back to the two gurneys once again ...

Dammit.

I momentarily leaned against a wall for support, and then pushed forward to examine the body bags. There was no identification on them visible, only a tag with a large red "C" that I assumed was their hospital code for a Covid death.

I reached for the zipper. It would just be a quick look at the face.

I have to know.

I vaguely heard the chime of an elevator door opening, and then a voice behind me asked, "Can I help you with something?"

I recognized the voice – Dr. Fleming – the ER

doc I spoke with three days earlier. I let go of the zipper slowly and turned to face him. It was time for some honesty.

"Dr. Fleming. I'm Dr. Spencer, from Ontario. I'm the husband of Sarah Spencer. We spoke on the phone Thursday night."

His surprise was evident, even through all of his protective gear. "Dr. Spencer? I'm shocked you made it here so quickly. You must have found a –"

"Doctor. My wife, Sarah. Is she –"

Just then, the door to the restroom, blocked by the body bag I was about to unzip, opened inward. Even through the mask, I recognized her face. I was stunned. My voice abandoned me and my legs turned to stone.

"Could someone help me move this damn gurney out of the way. I know I was in there a long time, but –"

"Of course, Mrs. Spencer. Let me help you." Dr. Fleming offered.

We both quickly moved the gurney to the side

as she stood in her hospital gown with one hand on the door frame and another on an IV pole. She was now looking directly at my face. With all the PPE I was wearing, she didn't seem to fully recognize me. Her head was cocked to one side as she said, "Thank you, Dr. Fleming. Who's your helper? He looks fam –"

I raised my face shield, stepped closer, looked her straight in the eyes, and whispered, "Sarah, you're ... okay?"

"Mark? Mark! It's you. What the hell are you doing here?" Her cheeks smiled under her mask as she wrapped me in an illegal hug, tears beginning to flow. My doctor instincts told me to pull away. She had Covid. But I couldn't, I needed to feel her.

"Dr. Spencer," Dr. Fleming said, "It's okay. Her second test just came back. Both were negative. She likely had a good case of garden-variety flu, with a little asthma exacerbation. She responded very quickly to the puffers and simple rehydration.

"We'll let her complete the 5-day course of azithromycin, but realistically she could be discharged anytime. She gave us quite a scare early on. We were just about to move her to the cold zone while we tried to contact you. I would have called you sooner, after the first test was negative, but we've had some false negatives, and I wanted to be sure ..."

Dr. Fleming went on for a while. Giving me an in-depth report, almost like he was signing a patient over to another physician. I didn't hear much after, "Both were negative." I was numb, like a cancer victim hearing their diagnosis for the first time. Except that this was good news. The best possible news.

"I'm sorry too, Mark, you must have been beside yourself with worry. I was completely out of it for 24 hours. When I woke up my phone was dead and with the precautions in place I couldn't get to my luggage and my charger. I wasn't even allowed to use a landline because I was in isolation. One of the nurses did try to call you at least once, yesterday."

When I was at the diner and had no reception.

My hand reached absentmindedly for the side

pocket of my scrub pants, where I would have stashed the Camodesivir, had I been able to hold on to it. All at once, I realized that my whole "Covid mission" really had been for nothing. I sank down into a chair near one of the gurneys. If I'd have stayed home, with Archie, Sarah might have hopped on a flight tomorrow morning and been home by evening. It was all for nothing.

Dr. Fleming looked at me, and said, "It appears you had a rough time getting here. I'm sure both of you have a lot of catching up to do. As I said, you can leave anytime. Your nurse will take care of the paperwork." He turned to Sarah. "It was a pleasure looking after you, Mrs. Spencer. Covid or not, I wish more of our patients showed your kind of recovery. It looks like you'll be in good hands to go home. Take care."

He bowed ever so slightly, turned, and briskly walked away, his open gown billowing like a cape in the wind. Sarah lowered herself onto my lap and lay her head on my shoulder. This drew stares from a few nurses, but I was too tired to care. Even through the mask, I could make out the fragrance of her hair – it smelled of home.

"You *don't* have Covid." I had to say it out loud, so that I could believe it.

"No, I don't."

"I really thought ... I really thought you might have ..."

"Mark." She turned now to catch my eye and hugged me hard.

"I knew you'd come for me."

***

Two days later, Sarah and I were sitting one seat apart on a plane heading directly to Toronto. I had the window and she had the aisle. Once again, we both had masks and gloves in place, and Sarah lathered sanitizer on every reachable surface. With the second and third waves coming, I presumed this would become the new norm for flying.

I was checking my phone before take-off and noticed an email reply from The Hitchhiker. I had sent off a furious email to the address on the back of his business card earlier this morning, not really expecting an answer. I stared at the screen for a moment, my finger poised over the delete button, deciding whether or not to open it. In the end, curiosity won the day, and I needed to know what the thief had to say for himself. There was no text. All the email contained was a link to a Pubmed article about Camodesivir. I pulled it up and read the abstract. It was published only two days earlier, and reported a 30% death rate in a large current COVID-19 trial. They had to crack the code to stop the study.

Son of a bitch. He knew. And was trying to stop me from potentially killing my wife.

I was still tired and recuperating from my journey. I would send him a reply and an apology when we landed in Toronto, telling him things couldn't have worked out better. I turned my head to look at my wife, my raison d'être. Life seemed different now that I thought I'd almost lost her, she seemed different. I stretched both arms out as much as I could, playfully messing with her hair in the process. She reached over and did the same, brushing her hand over my forehead, first giggling and then frowning. "Hey, you're a little on the warm side."

She reached up and adjusted the air conditioning. I turned to look out the window as we prepared for take-off and felt a strange tickle in my throat.

The End

AUTHOR'S NOTE

As mentioned in the subtitle, this is a work of fiction. That being said, most of the information, medical or otherwise, is real. The following are exceptions:

The medication Camodesivir does not exist, so don't go looking for it. It was made up as a combination of two drugs currently under investigation in the fight against COVID-19: Remdesivir and Camostat.

The diner in Knoxville is complete fabrication and was modeled after a restaurant I know in a small town called Blind River in Northern Ontario (also known from the Neil Young songs, Long May You Run and Helpless).

Florida was placed on Lockdown as of April, 3rd. Demonstrations against the lockdown did not occur until April, 19th. For timing and storytelling reasons, the small protest depicted in front of Cape Coral hospital in this story was entirely fictional, although the protest signs were real and taken from periods around the time of the lockdown protests, which were nationwide.

Acknowledgements

A special thanks to my wife, Andrea, for her encouragement, as well as to my children, Emily and Charles – always the first to read. A further thanks to my writing partner and old friend, Laura Cody – let the learning continue. A final thanks to author Cynthia Clement – for her detailed knowledge of the publishing process.

Of course, none of this would be possible without Connie and Murray Elder. Love you both dearly.

ABOUT THE AUTHOR

Graham Elder

Dr. Graham Elder was born in Montreal and attended McGill University for thirteen years, completing degrees in Physiotherapy, Medicine and Orthopaedic Surgery. He now lives with his wife and two children (when they are not at University) in the small town of Sault Ste. Marie in Northern Ontario, cresting the shorelines of beautiful Lake Superior, where he runs a busy surgical and academic practice with writing time divided between scientific publications and novels.

For other short stories and information about upcoming novels including The Epsilon Project (a collaboration with his writing partner, Laura Cody) please go to Twodocswriting.com.

This short novella came into being as a result of forced time off during the COVID-19 lockdown and is the consequence of an over active imagination somewhat constrained by the realities of science …

Learn more about the author at:
https://www.twodocswriting.com/about-graham-elder/
https://www.sootoday.com/arts-culture/graham-elders-grand-adventures-led-to-the-publication-of-a-novella-2780389

BOOKS IN THIS SERIES

A Covid Odyssey

Follow the world travels of Dr. Mark Spencer as he battles Covid-19.

A Covid Odyssey

A race against time to bring the cure for a deadly virus to a dying spouse.

Although the COVID-19 pandemic is ravaging the world, Dr. Mark Spencer's small town in Northern Ontario is largely unaffected other than being in lockdown and preparing for the potential onslaught. When his wife, Sarah – already attending a conference in Florida when the borders close – becomes deathly ill, she is admitted to a local hospital with minimal resources to treat Covid patients. As she spirals downward and with time running out, Mark concocts a plan to bring her an experimental anti-viral drug that might save her life. He must first, however, cross the Ontario/Michigan border and then travel 2000 km through a pandemic American landscape. Along his journey, he encounters a variety of unusual characters that bring into question the very foundation of his scientific beliefs.

Will Mark arrive at the hospital in time to save his wife?

No matter what, Mark's life will be forever changed by his Covid Odyssey.

A Covid Odyssey – Second Wave

A physician's harrowing intercontinental journey to uncover a dying father's potential cure for Covid-19.

Dr. Mark Spencer's life has finally returned to some degree of pandemic normalcy when he receives a heart-breaking phone call from his mother, who lives in England. His estranged father, a well-known virologist, has Covid and is being admitted to hospital.That same day, a letter arrives in the mailbox claiming that his father has discovered a cure for Covid-19, but that, for reasons unclear, Mark must go to England to retrieve it. Deciding that the possibility of a cure outweighs all else, Mark embarks on a gut-wrenching transatlantic trek that will ultimately push his resilience to the very limit.

Will Mark's treacherous voyage deliver him in time to uncover his father's secrets?

Join Dr. Spencer as he once again tackles the pandemic landscape in A Covid Odyssey – Second Wave.

Book two in the Amazon five-star trilogy: A Covid Odyssey

Manufactured by Amazon.ca
Bolton, ON